O.W.E. One World of Equals

Java Tales by Monica Somers

To order additional copies of this book, contact:
Xlibris Corporation
1-888-795-4274
www.Xlibris.com
Orders@Xlibris.com

It had been a long time since they last saw each other, but it was as if Mishka and Java had never been apart. After a quick game of tag in Java's backyard they decided to get ready to leave for the park. They were so excited to see the results of a year's worth of hard work.

Just as they were rounding the corner Schneider jumped out of the tree. He was a 1 month old squirrel who was interested in everything and everyone. "Schneider, don't jump out at people like that!" scolded Java. "Yeah, you almost scared the fur off of me!" added Mishka. "Sorry, sorry, but are you leaving now?" he asked full of excitement. "You betcha!" cheered Java. "Can you tell me the story again, huh, huh, huh?" begged Schneider. "Hop on my back and we will tell you as we walk over" said Mishka as she walked under the giant green Oak tree and let the baby squirrel hop on.

"Well, you see, Java and I have both had to live our lives with disabilities and with that comes the starring and finger pointing," Mishka said sadly. "Yeah and it even happens to people who are not disabled, but have other differences," added Java. "O.W.E. was started for all of us and happened one day when Java and I were playing down at the park" Mishka said. She had such excitement and hope in her voice that Schneider's bright orange hair began to puff out all around his tail.

"It was the first day of spring and a beautiful one at that, so Java and I decided not to let it go to waste." Java slowed down and turned toward Mishka and Schneider who were slowly creeping out from behind the fence. "As we were playing, different animals in the park began to yell, point and laugh at us," added Java. "There is one thing in life you always have to remember Schneider" said Mishka "and that is never put up with people making you feel bad about yourself.

When Java noticed that the bull dog from next store was pointing at us she stopped and said "This is it!" You could see the shock on Montgomery's face as the 3 legged cat approached him. Excuse me Montgomery, but why is it that you make such fun of Mishka and me? Have we ever done anything that hurt your feelings or made you mad?" she asked of their neighbor.

Mishka interrupted quickly and said "Montgomery had no idea what to say at first because he was so shocked that someone had called him out. He began to hem and haw and then he told us the one thing that started this whole club." "What was that, tell me, tell me?" pleaded Schneider. "He said that he had no idea!" exclaimed Java. Schneider's eyes grew huge and he shook with such shock that he fell right off of Mishka. "Ahhh! Schneider are you okay?" questioned Mishka. "I'm fine, I just don't understand how you can dislike someone so very much and then not even have a reason."

As they reached the general store on the corner of their road, Java paused and turned towards Mishka and her riding companion. "You see Schneider, that is the thing with the **great dislike** . . . it comes from so long ago that the people who own it don't even know why.

"So what did Montgomery finally say?" Schneider questioned as he scratched his right ear. "He said" began Mishka when suddenly a loud grumbly voice interrupted, "I said I don't know. I just know that dogs and cats do not like each other," said Montgomery sternly. "MONTGOMMERY!" screamed Mishka as she ran over and squeezed him hello. "Are you ready?" asked Montgomery, "of course, can you believe it was one year ago today?" added Java.

Montgomery went to answer Java when Schneider ran up on top of Mishka's head, "wait, wait, wait don't ruin the story by telling me the ending now!" begged the fuzzy baby squirrel. "Oh, pardon me . . . where were you guys?" "I was just about to tell Schneider how we suddenly realized that the **great dislike** really had nothing to do with us, our disabilities or our friendships. As a matter of fact, most of the animals who had made fun of us didn't even know us. They were all making fun and teasing because they followed what they had heard or were told or were taught.

Montgomery shook his head to rid his mouth of the slimy drool that hung around his big bull dog lips and then sat down for a minute. "You see little guy, that day we were so shocked that we decided to go and ask others why they disliked each other. What started as a simple question sparked such a magical change!"

Mishka sat down next to Montgomery and motioned to Java to rest along side her. "We asked Remy, the cat that lives at the general store, why she had big dislike for Fred, the mouse who lived in the back of the general store. "What did he say, huh, huh, huh?" begged Schneider. "He said he wasn't quite sure, but his father told him, as his father had years ago, that cats were supposed to chase and eat birds and . . ." "MICE!" screamed Fred, interrupting Java as he climbed out of the basement boards that were coming loose in the back of the store. "Hi ya Fred!" exclaimed everyone at once. "Hi all!" responded Fred.

"Can you believe that once Remy and I talked we actually liked each other and had a lot of things in common!" said Fred. "Yeah" cheered Remy "and now we are best friends." Schneider couldn't believe what he was hearing. "So where does **great dislike** come from?" questioned the curious little squirrel. "We aren't quite sure, but we know that once the animals who had **great dislike** for each other spoke they became friends and could not find a reason for it. "This is where our club **O.W.E.** came from!" cheered Mishka.

After the five of us began to talk we all decided that we were just as bad as the animals who started the **great dislike**. "Huh, how is it that you figure that?" asked the puzzled little squirrel. "Because we just followed along with it!" said the three-legged cat. "Weren't you scared?" Schneider curiously questioned her. "That's the thing, you can never allow fear to get in the way of the truth or change. Everything changes like the trees, but it's all of our jobs to make sure that the change is for the better.

"So on that day, right over there in the park, Mishka had stepped on a stick. Thank goodness that Remy knew where the store owner had his band aides. The minute she put it on her foot we knew what it meant." "Uh, I guess that I am confused" stated Schneider. "Didn't it mean that she was hurt? "YES!" cheered the gang. Putting his arm around the squirrel, Montgomery added "We all thought, band aides fix booboos so why not fix the **great dislike**. On that day, each one of us decided to put on a band aide and start helping the world to find friends and happiness in new places."

As she finished cleaning her front paw, Java exclaimed "And we named our club **O.W.E.**, which means **O**ne **W**orld of **E**quals!"

"Then we all decided to set out in our normal lives and pass on the word," said Mishka. Everyone is supposed to meet back here today so that we can see how far our message has traveled" Fred happily added. "Are we ready gang?" questioned Mishka as they all stood up to enter the park.

"What if no one is here, what if our message went no where?" asked a puzzled and somewhat scared Montgomery. "Well, we will be disappointed, but at least we know that we tried, that is a lot better than being unhappy and just putting up with it," added Java. "You betcha!" said Fred as he jumped onto Remy's back. "What we discovered is that it is always harder to stand up for what is right then to live with the way things are. Easier is not always better."

The nervous group of six brave animals started crossing the street to the park when suddenly Schneider screamed "LOOK!" They could not believe their eyes. The park was full! Full of different animals from all around the world and they were all wearing **O.W.E.** band aides.

"We did!" they cheered at once. "We sure did!" exclaimed Mishka, as she led the gang into the park. There were alligators next to deer and lions laughing along with a nearby group of gorillas. There were animals that were disabled and then there were sworn enemies sitting together!

All the animals in the park shared their stories that night and they all had the same basic discovery . . . they actually liked the animals that they were supposed to dislike or fight with.

After the huge celebration, the six excited and now very tired friends sat down to talk about the day's events. "As great as this is though we must not stop . . . change is alive and we have to continue to help others understand. We cannot let the "**GREAT DISLIKE**" win" added Java. "You're right Java, one animal at a time, one nice gesture, or even one straightened out misunderstanding." added Remy.

"We will continue our mission . . . We will continue to let others know about the "**GREAT DISLIKE**" cheered Schneider. Everyone was exhausted and proud. While they all knew that their work was not done, they relaxed and rejoiced, for they had made a difference!

This book is dedicated to both my parents and my two children.  To my parents who never allowed me to accept the way things were.  Through their love and support they have gifted me the ability to challenge.  To challenge myself, as well as the world around me.  To always attempt to see the good in people, even if they are unable to see it in themselves.  In doing so, they have given me the ability to see magic in even the tiniest good deed.

To my children, Hanna and Mekhi, for putting the color back into my world!  They have enabled me to truly find happiness and contentment in just enjoying life.  My heart will always beat one time extra for all of them.

Printed in the United States
By Bookmasters